LEGO SUPER HEROES

BRICK ADVENTURES
3 NEW ACTION-PACKED, ILLUSTRATED STORIES!

SUPER-VILLAIN GHOST SCARE!

SCHOLASTIC INC.

ISBN 978-1-338-26051-9

10 9 8 7 6 5 4 3 2 1   18 19 20 21 22

Printed in the U.SA.   40
First printing 2018

Book design by Erin McMahon

CONTENTS

FRIENDS OF THE FLASH YOU WILL MEET

BATMAN:
A Super Hero who lives in Gotham City. Batman is really Bruce Wayne.

SUPERMAN:
A Super Hero who can fly, heat things with his eyes, and cool things with his breath, and is super-strong.

BATGIRL:
A Super Hero who lives in Gotham City, Barbara Gordon fights crime as Batgirl.

SUPERGIRL:
A Super Hero who has super-strength and super-speed like her cousin, Superman.

INTRODUCTION

HI THERE! ARE YOU READY FOR A GHOST STORY? ACTUALLY, *THREE* GHOST STORIES! SEE, SOMETIMES REALLY STRANGE THINGS HAPPEN IN CENTRAL CITY, WHERE I LIVE. I'M PRETTY SMART, BUT I NEVER WOULD HAVE FIGURED OUT THIS WEIRD STUFF ON MY OWN. GOOD THING I CAN ALWAYS CALL MY FRIENDS IN THE JUSTICE LEAGUE!

SPOOKY CASE #1

TRICK OR THIEF?

It was Halloween in **Central City**, where **The Flash**, the Justice League's hero with super-speed, lives. Kids in costumes ran all over the city, trick-or-treating. A group of friends in a quiet neighborhood already had sacks full of candy, but they wanted to knock on the door of one last house. They remembered there was a house at the end of their block that they hadn't been to yet. Maybe they would have candy there? They ran around the corner and came to a quick stop.

The old house they remembered was gone! In its place was a big, creepy house with broken windows and paint that was peeling off the sides. The kids thought it was very weird this dusty old **mansion** had popped up out of nowhere. But they wanted candy and started to walk up to the front door. Then, slowly, the doorknob started to turn . . .

"*AAAAAAH!*" the kids screamed, and they ran away as fast as they could. As they ran down the street they ran past a man in costume—it was The Flash! He had just returned to Central City from an adventure with his friends in the **Justice League**.

Wow, I know Halloween is scary, but those kids seem really scared! he thought.

He looked at the old mansion the kids were running from. He had just been on this street last week and knew the block well. "Hey . . . I don't remember a mansion being here! Hmm . . ." He walked up to the front door of the mansion and looked around.

"Well," he said, hopping from foot to foot, "this sure is a big, scary old house. Hmm . . . maybe I shouldn't go in alone." He tapped his Justice League **communicator**, a special earpiece he had that let him talk to his Super Hero friends. "Hey, uh, does anyone want to come to Central City to see a big, creepy mansion that seems to have come out of nowhere?"

"Do I ever!" **Batgirl** responded.

"I admit, I am also . . . interested," said **Batman**.

"Oh, yeah, Batman, this is totally your kind of place!" The Flash said.

"We'll be right there," Batgirl answered.

After a few minutes, Batgirl and Batman arrived. Batgirl, Batman, and The Flash opened the door to the mansion slowly. The house was full of dusty furniture and had cobwebs on the ceiling. There were old, tattered books on bookcases. Batman and Batgirl crept into the room, followed by The Flash, who was very scared.

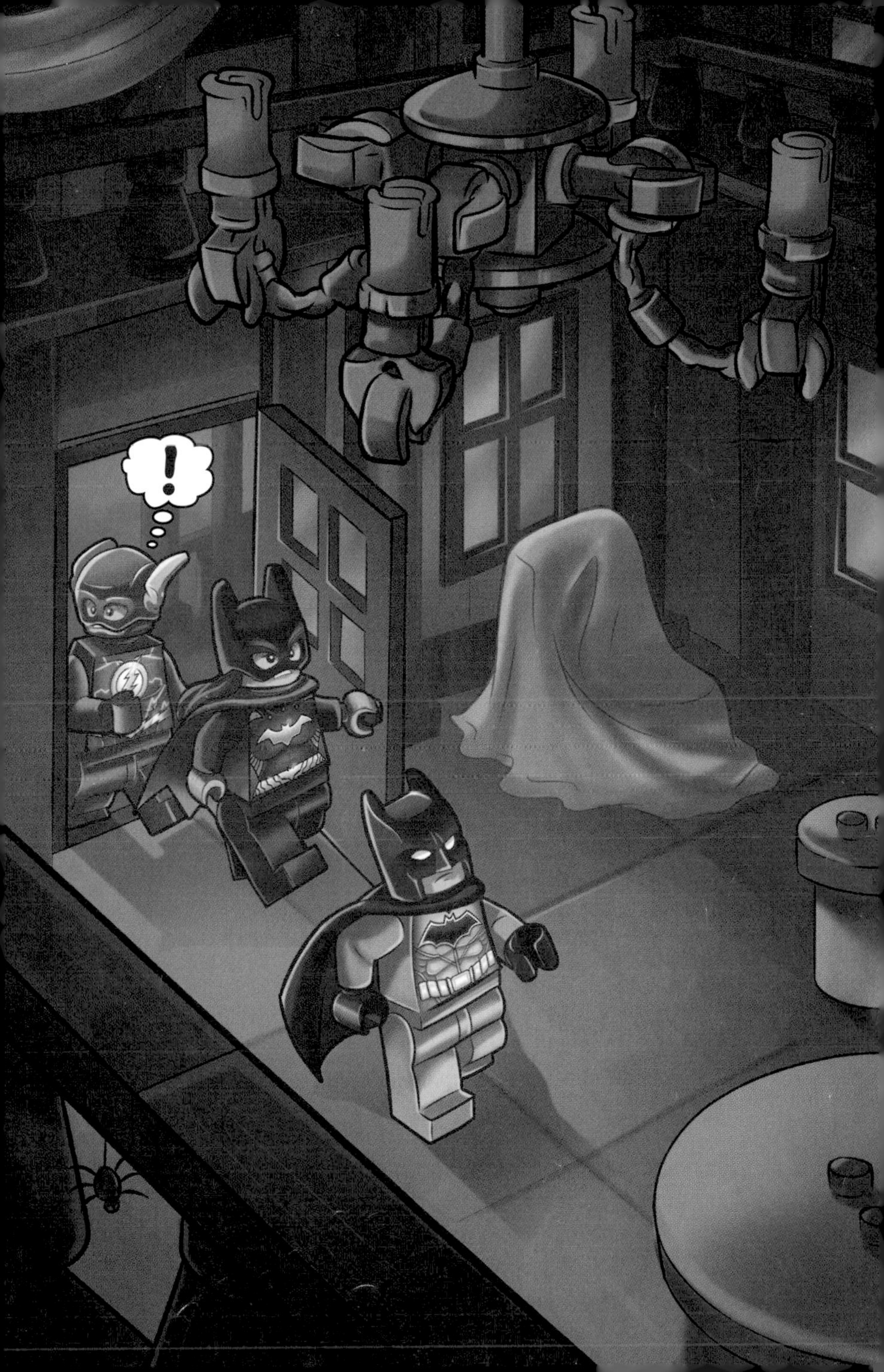
!

Batman drew a line through the dust on a coffee table. "This place looks really old . . ."

A rush of air moved through the room, and *SLAM!* The front door shut behind them. The heroes all turned toward it.

"*Easy*, Flash," said Batgirl. "I know you're nervous, but—"

"I didn't slam that door!" cried The Flash.

"Well, it wasn't me," Batgirl said. "I was listening to Batman."

"And it wasn't me," said Batman. He looked back down at the dusty table. "Hmm . . ."

Batgirl and The Flash came over for a closer look. Instead of a straight line drawn through the dust on the table, a message was now spelled out: LEAVE.

"Um, so," The Flash said, "I—I'm guessing you didn't, uh, write that? Batman?"

"No."

"Okay, well then, I think it's clear that *we are standing inside a haunted house! MAYBE WE SHOULD—*"

"*Flash*," Batman barked, cutting him off, "there's no such thing as ghosts."

"But someone wants us to *think* this house is haunted," added Batgirl, pulling out her phone.

The Flash took a few fast, deep breaths. "Sure, right. Ha ha, I was *kidding*. 'Haunted house.' Ha! No such thing! I'm not scared at all. So, how do we—"

Another rush of air, and *thump*! *Thunk!* Book after book came flying off the bookshelf and landed on the wooden floor.

"YAH!" yelped The Flash, jumping into Batman's arms.

"Well, while you were busy *not* being scared"—said Batgirl with a giggle—"I was recording." Batgirl held up her phone.

"You *recorded* that?" The Flash hopped off Batman, who adjusted his cape.

"Well, yeah," Batgirl replied. "I think I got a good video of the bookshelf, too. Let's see." She tapped on her phone a few times to rewind the **footage**. "Aha!"

Batman and The Flash looked over Batgirl's shoulders at the video. She paused it just before the books fell off the shelf. There was an orange blur in the video.

"Look how fast that's moving," murmured Batgirl. "What is it?"

"Not 'what,' 'who'! That's a speedster!" The Flash said. "So *that's* how this house was built so fast," he said. "Someone used their super-speed to build it!"

"And now they're using their super-speed to make the house seem haunted!" finished Batgirl. "But why?"

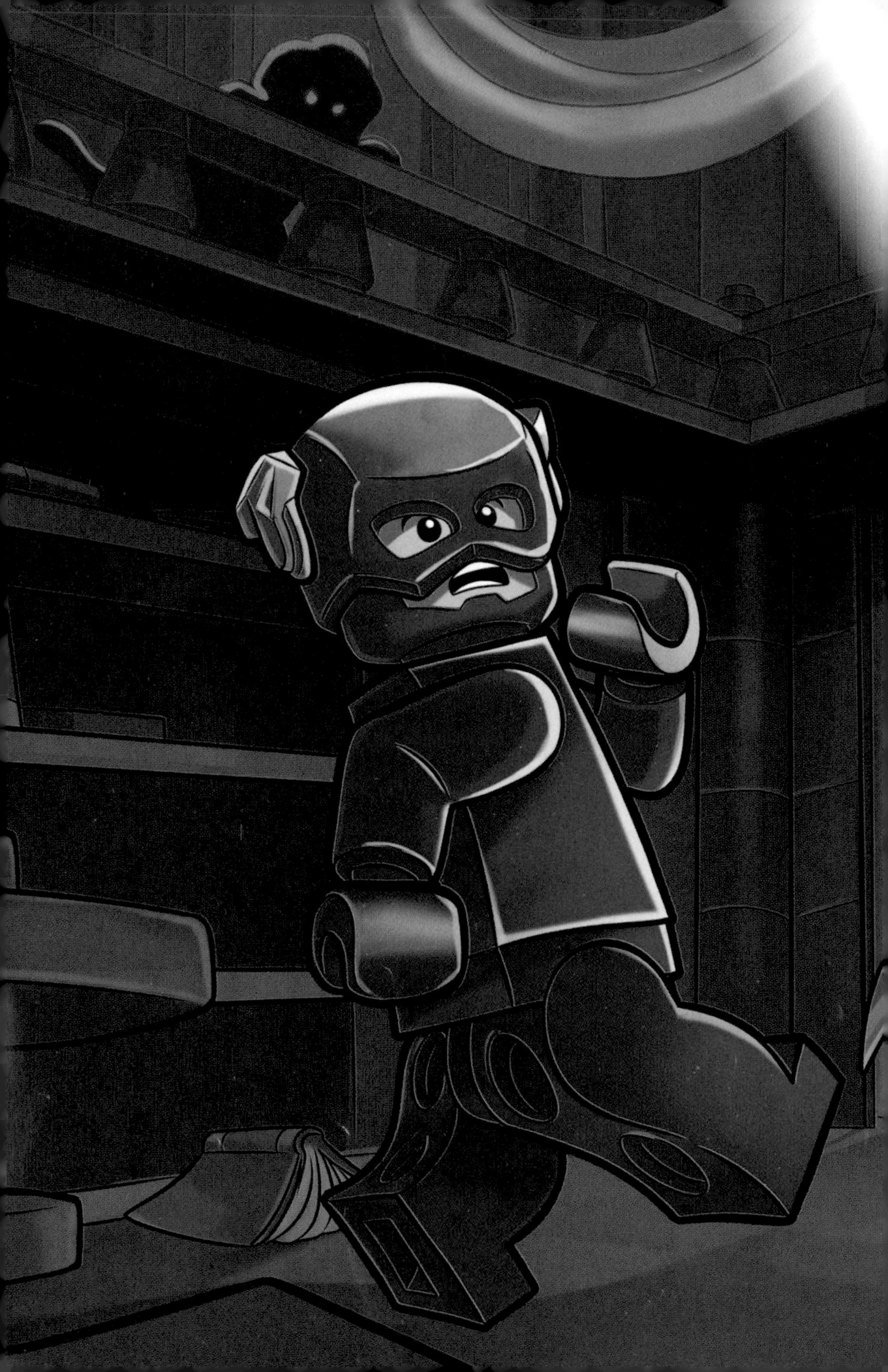

The Flash clapped his hands decisively. "Let's catch 'em quick so we can ask 'em!" The heroes got together and whispered a plan to one another. After a few minutes, they started walking to the door . . .

"Too bad we couldn't catch that ghost!" Batgirl called back over her shoulder.

"Yeah, guess we'll just have to give up!" The Flash yelled.

There was a pause, and then Batgirl elbowed Batman.

"Oh!" Batman said, very loudly and awkwardly. "Yes! It is a shame that we could not bring this bad guy ghost to justice!"

Batgirl rolled her eyes and pulled the door shut behind her.

A few seconds passed in the empty room. Then a rush of air and a blur moved toward the door. As it passed over the fallen books, there was a click and a *whoosh*. Books flew into the air, and then someone was swinging upside down from the ceiling!

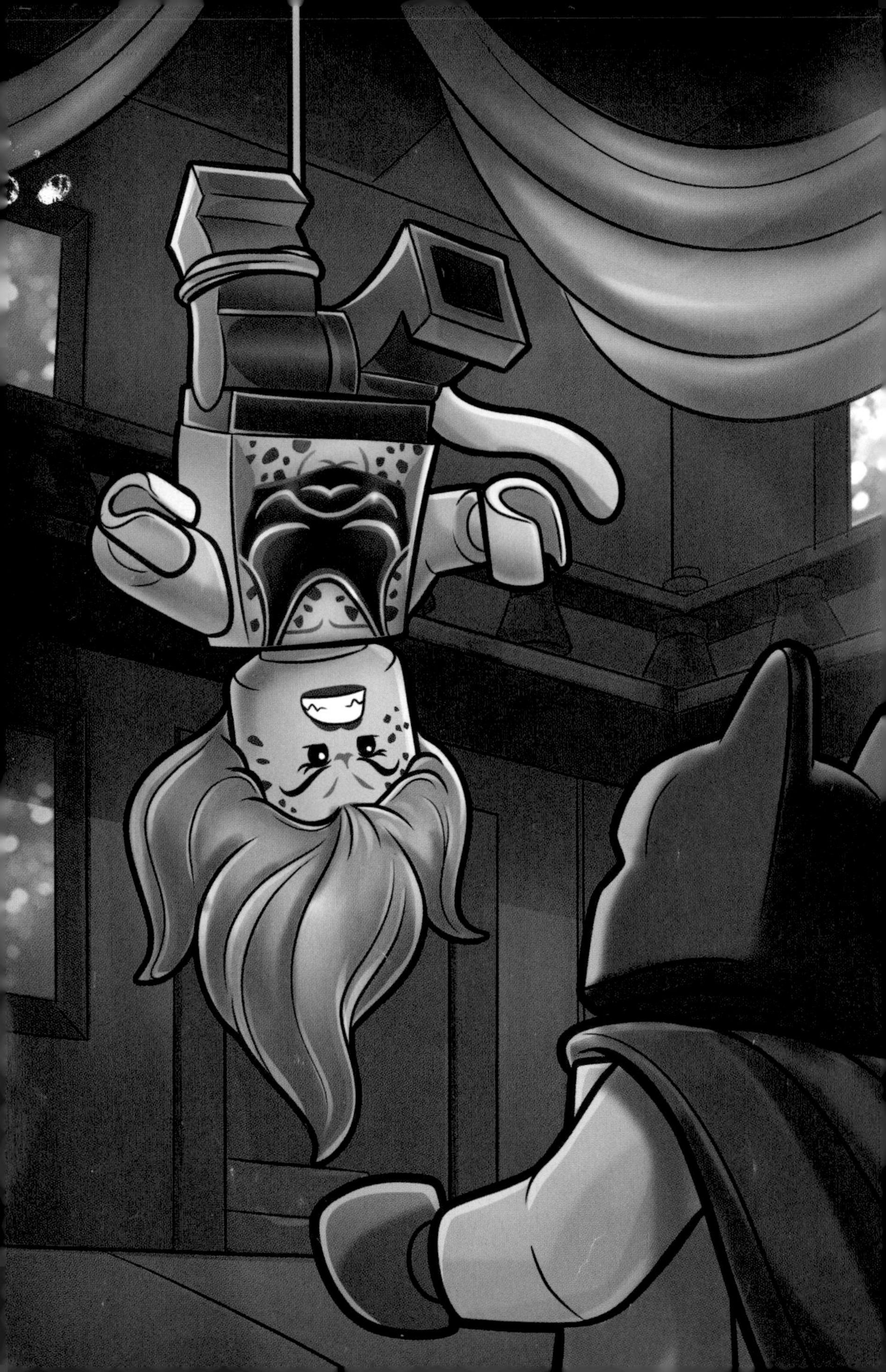

BANG! The front door burst open, and the heroes ran in. There, hanging by her ankle from a Batman booby trap, was one of the Justice League's enemies: **Cheetah**! With super-strength and speed, she was half-woman, half-cheetah, and an all-around super-villain!

"You stepped into that trap faster than I thought!" said Batgirl, smiling.

"Cheetah," Batman said sternly, "what are you up to in this house?"

Cheetah sighed. "I needed someplace safe to hide all"—she paused—"all my stuff."

"You mean all your *stolen loot*?" Batgirl corrected.

"Yes, fine!" Cheetah snarled. "So I built the scariest-looking house I could, and I made everyone think it was haunted so no one would use it as a hideout. No one was supposed to come here!" She frowned at them. "How did you even set this trap? I was watching you. You had no time!"

"Cheetah," said The Flash proudly, "maybe you can be as spooky as a ghost. But *no one* is faster than The Flash!"

SPOOKY CASE #2

GROCERY STORE GHOSTS

It was early in the morning, but The Flash was already hard at work. A Central City grocery store had been robbed overnight!

The Flash was pointing to some puddles of water, talking to the grocery store manager. "This is *really* the only clue?"

The grocery store manager shrugged. "Those," she said, "and that." She pointed at the spicy food section, where all the shelves had been cleaned out. "Whoever—or *whatever*—did this? They took everything."

The Flash stood up. "What do you mean, 'whatever'?"

"Well"—said the manager nervously—"this is the third grocery store this has happened to. Every time, there's nothing left behind except these weird puddles of water, and the thieves just take all the hot sauce and spicy food.

All the tacos, hot peppers, and salsas are gone! Every time, the security cameras stop working right before things disappear. And every time"—she shivered—"when everyone gets to work the next morning, the whole store is freezing!"

"Oh," The Flash said, "it's not normally this cold in here? I thought you just liked it chilly!"

"No! It's creepy!" The manager leaned in and whispered, "Some of us think it may be . . . well, some sort of g-g-g-ghost!"

"A ghost?!" The Flash asked.

"Shh!" She was embarrassed but went on. "I've heard of ghosts who haunt places to cause trouble or get revenge. Maybe this is the spirit of someone who really liked spicy food? Or maybe—"

"Hoo, okay," interrupted The Flash. "Uh . . . be right back." He darted outside and activated his Justice League communicator. "Haunted grocery store! Haunted grocery store!" he yelled.

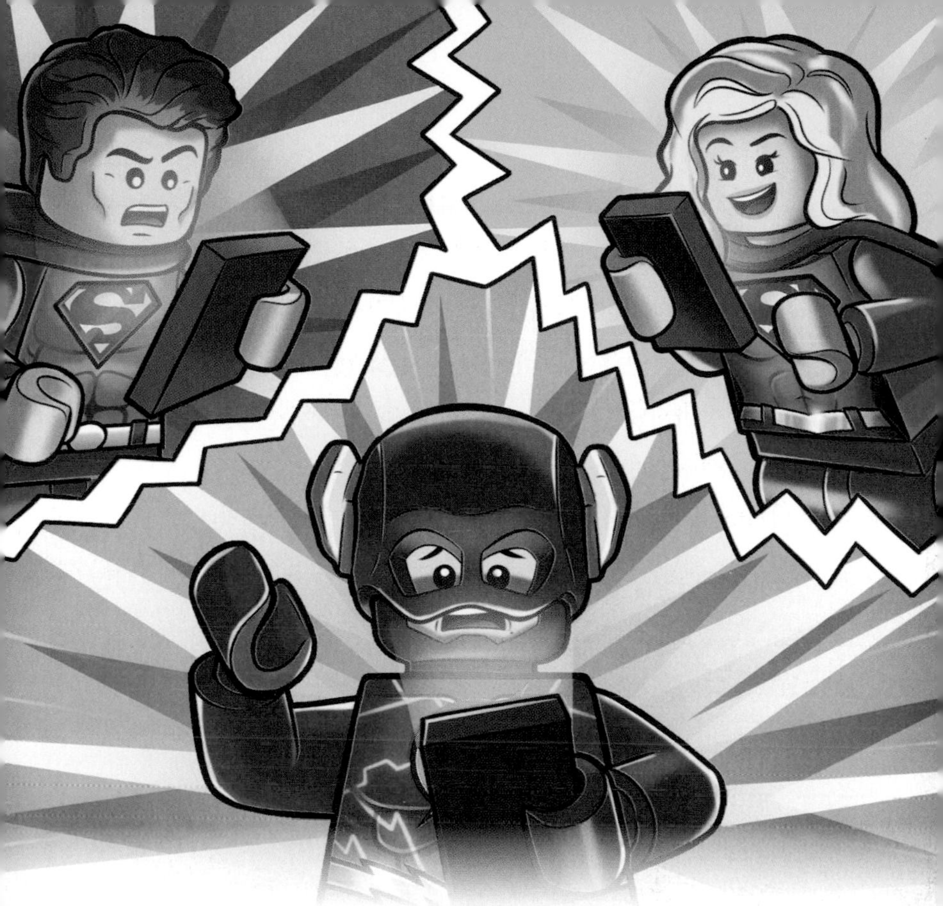

“. . . Hello? Flash, is that you?” came **Superman**’s voice.

“Yes! Also *haunted grocery store*!”

“Neato!” responded **Supergirl**. “We’ll be right there!”

A little while later, Superman and Supergirl arrived at the store. The Flash showed them the puddles of water. "See?" he said. "Creepy puddles, missing spicy food, and the air is always chilly? It's a spicy taco ghost!"

"Not necessarily, Flash," said Superman. "Cold can mean lots of things, not just ghosts."

"Yeah, watch!" said Supergirl. She blew a frosty breath at a shelf nearby, turning it into a giant ice cube.

"Exactly." Superman nodded. "Our freeze breath is enough to stop any villain in their tracks. Until it melts, of course. And there's nothing ghostly about it!"

"Wait, 'melts,'" said The Flash. "That's it!" He raced from puddle to puddle, looking up at the grocery store ceiling. "Look! These puddles are all under the security cameras!"

Supergirl flew up to the nearest camera and opened a panel on the side. Water flooded out and splashed right into The Flash's face.

"Ack!" he cried. "It's freezing!"

"No, you were right the first time," Superman said. "It's *melting*. Someone froze the cameras to make them stop working, and then the ice melted and made these puddles. We're looking for a thief who can control ice!"

That night, Superman, Supergirl, and The Flash hid in the next largest grocery store in the neighborhood. Superman and Supergirl flew up into the shadows near the ceiling, and The Flash crouched behind a long counter. They didn't have to wait long before . . .

Crackle! Crackle! Crackle! Beams of ice shot out and froze the security cameras. Then a familiar figure stepped into the center of the room.

"**Killer Frost**!" shouted Supergirl, flying down out of the shadows. "See, Flash? She's no ghost!"

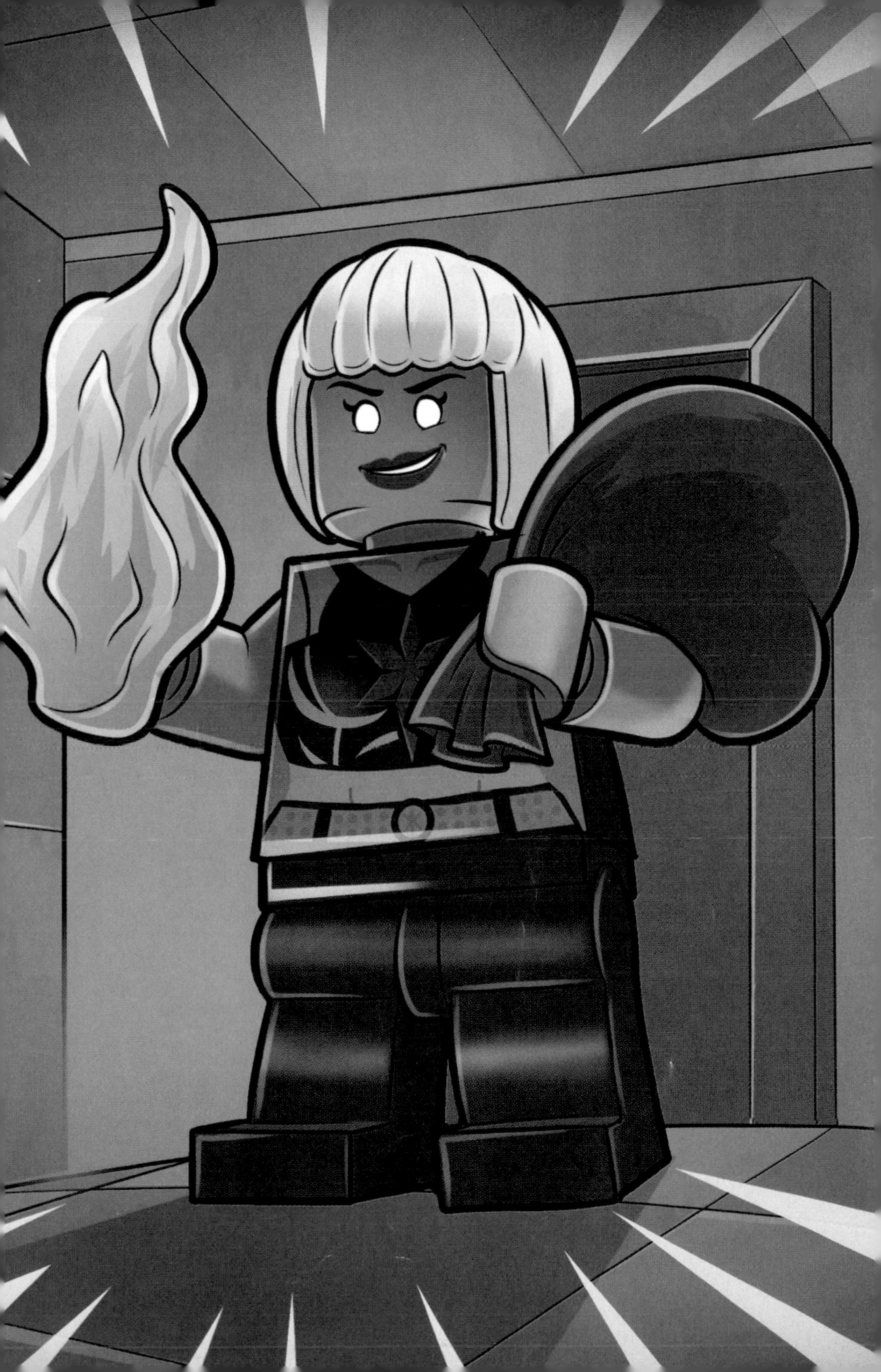

Killer Frost laughed. "You thought I was a ghost? Ha!" She raised her hands and blasted a wave of frost at Supergirl.

Supergirl dodged the blast. "Ooh, so *rude*!" she said. Her eyes glowed red, and a ray of **heat vision** blasted out at Killer Frost.

"Good idea, Supergirl! This ought to warm her up," said Superman, striking out with his own heat vision.

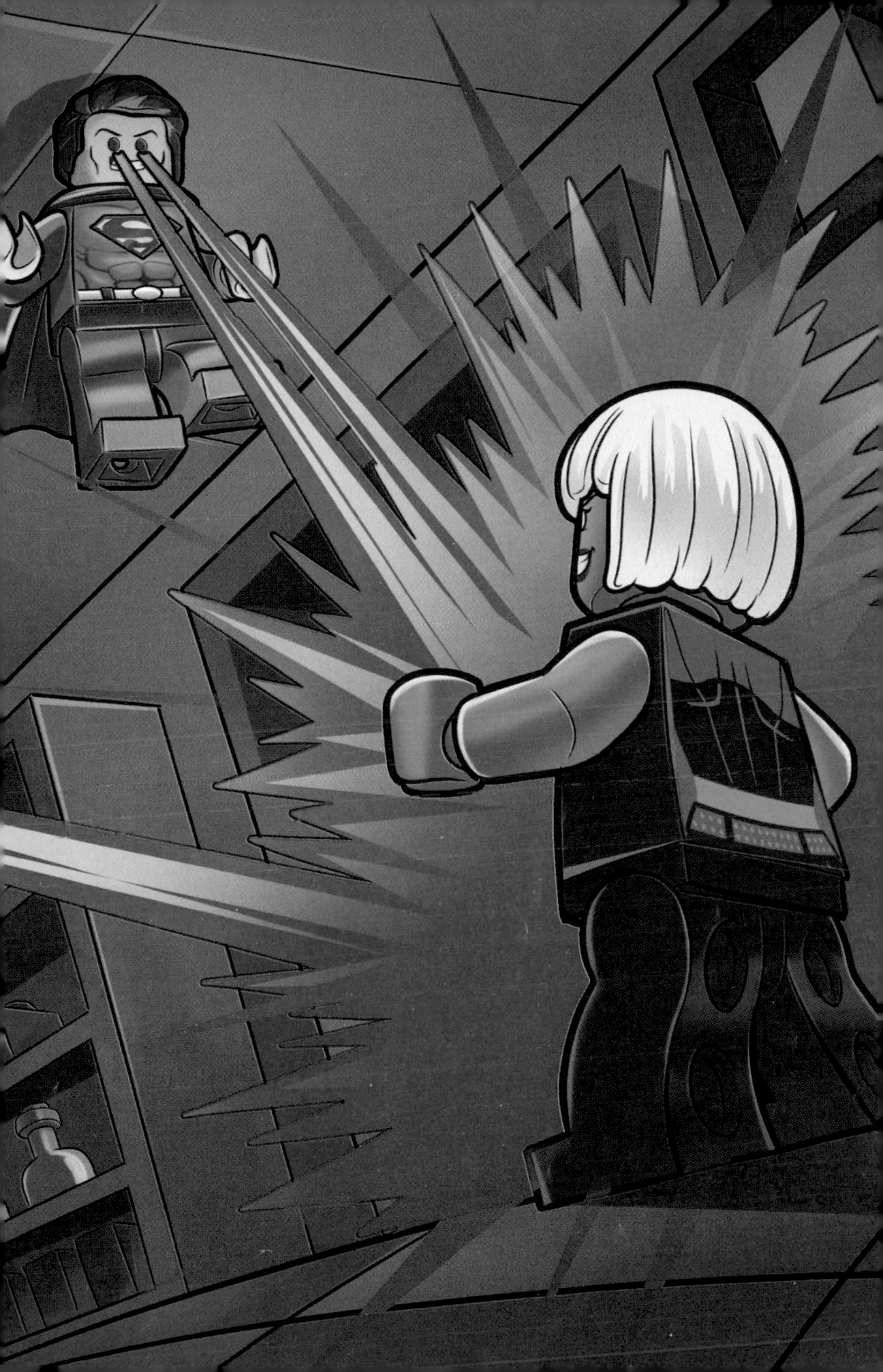

To the heroes' surprise, Killer Frost didn't seem to mind the heat rays. "Thanks for the pick-me-up," she said with a laugh.

"Wait!" called The Flash. "I just remembered: Killer Frost *absorbs* heat energy. It makes her stronger, not weaker! That's why she was stealing hot sauce and spicy foods!"

"Aw, come on!" said Killer Frost, turning her ice beam toward The Flash.

The Flash jumped to the side, and the beam shot by him. "I have an idea to get the heat energy back out of her," he said. "Follow me!"

The Flash ran at Killer Frost, moving from side to side to avoid the beams. He ran around her, faster and faster, spinning her in circles. Finally, he ran away and turned back to look.

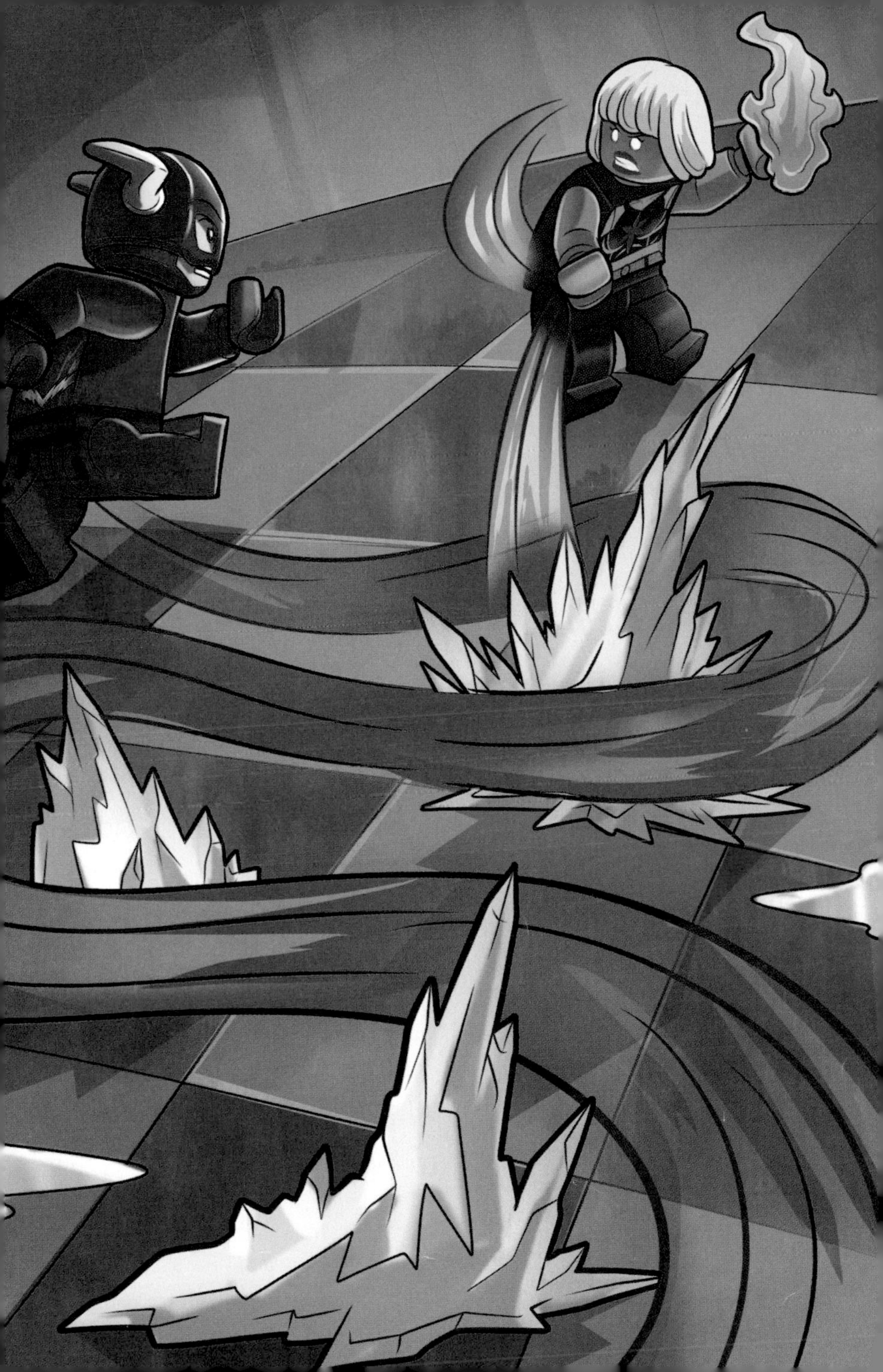

Killer Frost stood on her feet, dizzy, holding her head with one hand. With the other hand, she tried to fire her ice beams at the heroes. But the beams were much smaller now, and she was so dizzy  that her aim was terrible, firing blocks of ice all around the room.

Superman and Supergirl flew down, knocking Killer Frost off-balance so she fell to her knees. Then The Flash grabbed the ice blocks and, before Killer Frost could blink, built them into a pile all around her.

"Ugh," grumbled Killer Frost, "you are the *worst*, Flash."

"Hey, don't be like that." The Flash chuckled. "Maybe being in jail will give you time to *warm up* to me."

A DAY AT THE MUSEUM

"I gotta admit, Flash," whispered Batgirl, "when you said your museum was being attacked by ghosts, I had my doubts. But . . ."

Batgirl, Batman, Superman, Supergirl, and The Flash were crouched by the huge statue of The Flash in front of The **Flash Museum**. The Flash Museum was in his home of Central City and contained trophies from his past adventures. Carefully, Batgirl peeked around the base of the statue and looked at the building again.

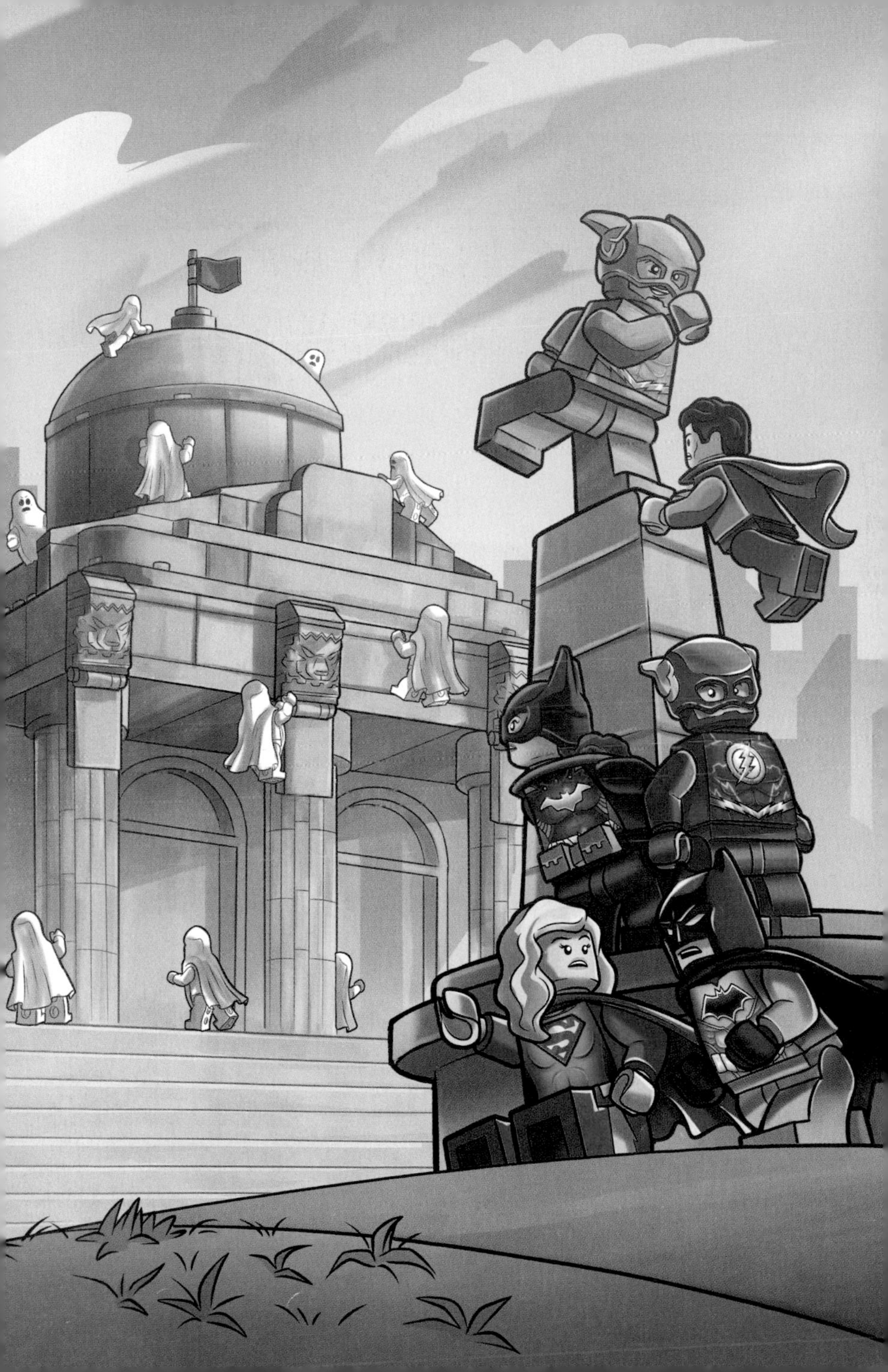

"Yup," she finished. "Those definitely look like ghosts!"

Dozens of white-sheeted figures were climbing all over the outside of the museum.

"And they're trying to get inside," added Batman. "If they succeed, they could steal or break many valuable **exhibits**—"

"Including the **Cosmic Treadmill**!" The Flash looked alarmed. "Batman and I built that to travel through time. It's way too powerful to let any thieves get their hands on it."

He stopped and frowned. "Wait. Do ghosts have hands?"

"Let's find out!" Supergirl took flight and sped off toward one of the ghosts on the roof. Superman followed her.

WHAM! She punched the ghost in the face, and it spun around. It lashed out with one of its arms and knocked into Supergirl.

"Aw, you're so cute when you're wobbly!" Supergirl laughed.

The ghost stopped moving. It began to vibrate and glow with a creepy light. Then, to Supergirl's surprise, it hit her with a super-strong punch!

"Hey, I felt that!" she cried. The rest of the ghosts on the roof turned to look at her. One by one, they began to vibrate and glow.

"I'm coming!" called Superman. He flew toward the ghost that had punched Supergirl. *BANG!* He knocked it straight off the edge of the building, and the heroes watched as it fell. To their surprise, when it hit the ground, it sparked!

Superman and Supergirl flew down to get a better look. The ghost wasn't moving, and underneath the sheet they saw a tangle of metal and wires.

"Friends, I think these 'ghosts' are just robots," reported Superman. "But they look very high-tech. Who knows what they can do?"

"Well, they can't fly. That's good," said Supergirl. "But I think they get stronger when they glow."

Batman tapped his chin thoughtfully. "If they're robots, then someone must be telling them to do this."

"Maybe we can figure out who!" said Batgirl. "Superman, Supergirl, Flash: You keep the robots from breaking in while Batman and I search for the signal that's controlling them."

"On it!" The Flash ran for the museum doors. He snatched up one of the ghosts, ran with it straight up the side of the building, and then dropped it. *SMASH!* "One down!" he yelled, already running back toward the entrance.

"Watch out for the glowing ones!" Superman called. He and Supergirl flew off to help.

Batman pulled a gadget with a long **antenna** out of his belt and switched it on. "Scanning . . ." he muttered. The device started beeping. "Aha! I've got the signal that someone is sending these ghost robots, and it seems to be coming from the museum. But I can't find exactly where."

"I can help," said Batgirl, running around the side of the building. She pulled out her phone and tapped it a few times. "I found the signal, too. Connecting with your device . . . there."

"Good thinking, Batgirl. When our two devices team up, we can get a better sense of exactly where—wait."

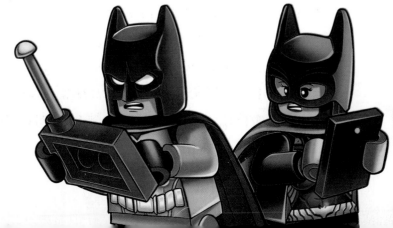

The device started beeping faster, then, with a *ping!*, all the lights on it turned green.

"That's weird," Batgirl said. "Is the signal coming from . . . the museum basement?"

"Justice League," Batman said into his communicator. "The bad guy is already inside the museum. These 'ghosts' are just a trick!"

"Then they're good at their job!" yelled The Flash. He was being grabbed by five glowing ghosts at once. "I'm very tricked!"

"Flash, get inside and find out what's going on," instructed Batman. "The rest of us can handle things out here."

"You got it, Batman." The Flash opened the museum door and ran through it. Some ghost robots inside tried to grab him again, but he was too fast for them, and ran down the stairs to the basement.

Ahead of him, he heard the sound of someone complaining, and every once in a while a *BANG*. He slowed down and poked his head around the corner quietly.

Bent over the Cosmic Treadmill, adjusting something with a wrench, was **Reverse-Flash**!

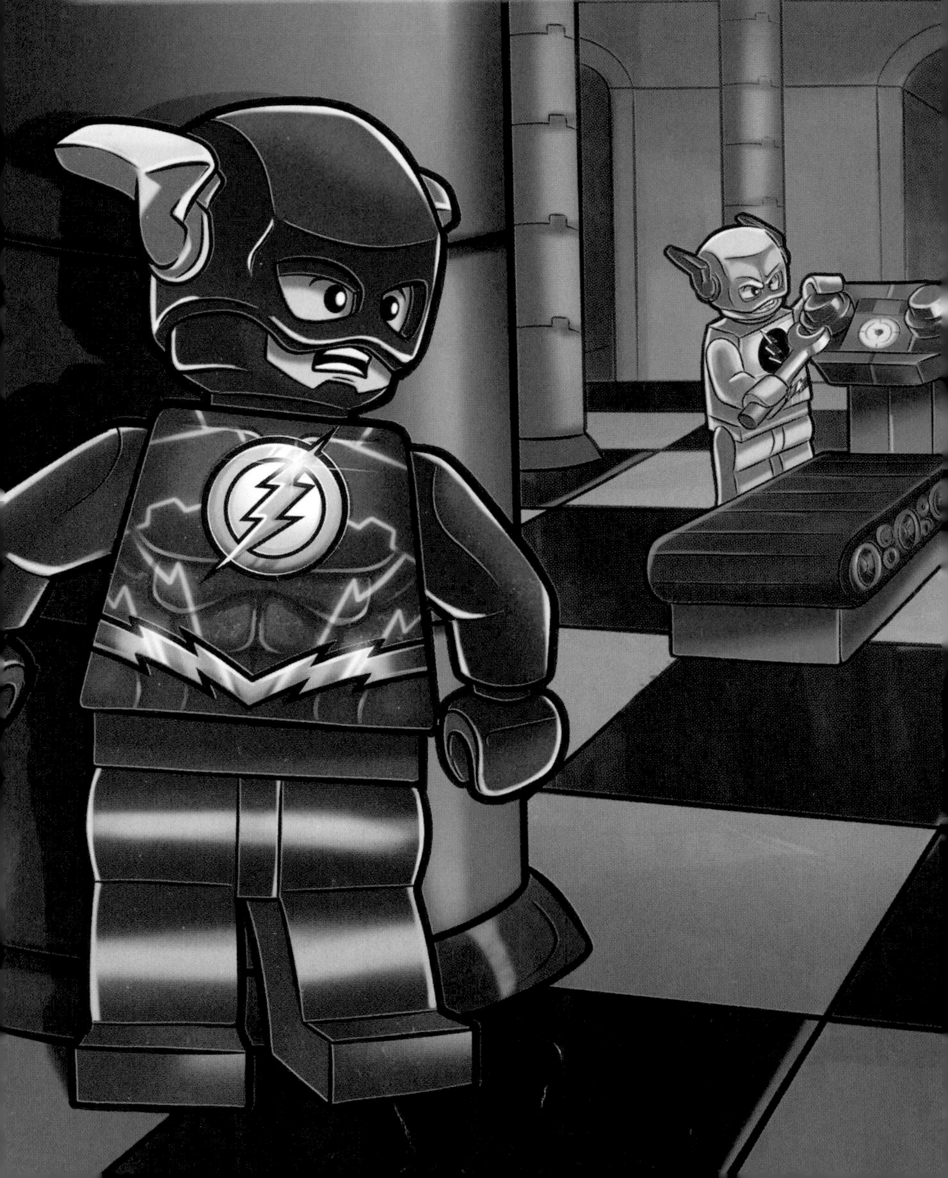

Reverse-Flash was one of The Flash's enemies—he was from the future, wore a yellow suit that looked like The Flash's suit, and had super-speed. As The Flash watched, Reverse-Flash struggled to loosen one of the bolts along the side of the treadmill.

"Arrrrgh!" Reverse-Flash growled to himself. "Why won't it work? This technology is so hard to use! Of course, after I use this treadmill to travel to the past and stop the Justice League from ever being created, I won't have to worry! Heh heh heh."

"Reverse-Flash is here!" The Flash whispered into his communicator.

"Aha!" Batman responded. "That's why these robots are so advanced. Reverse-Flash must have made them from technology he brought with him from the future!"

"I have an idea," said Batgirl. "Flash, give us five minutes, and then lead Reverse-Flash out the front door."

"Okay. I've got a plan."

The Flash raced across the room, straight past Reverse-Flash, and yanked the control panel off the Cosmic Treadmill.

"Can't time travel without this, buddy!" The Flash teased, waving the control panel over his head. "Come and get it!" He raced up the stairs and into the main exhibit hall.

Reverse-Flash yelled out and ran after him at top speed. On the main floor, he saw The Flash standing in the doorway to the **Hall of Heroes**, a part of the museum filled with real-looking statues of Super Heroes and super-villains. The Flash ran into the Hall, with Reverse-Flash right behind him.

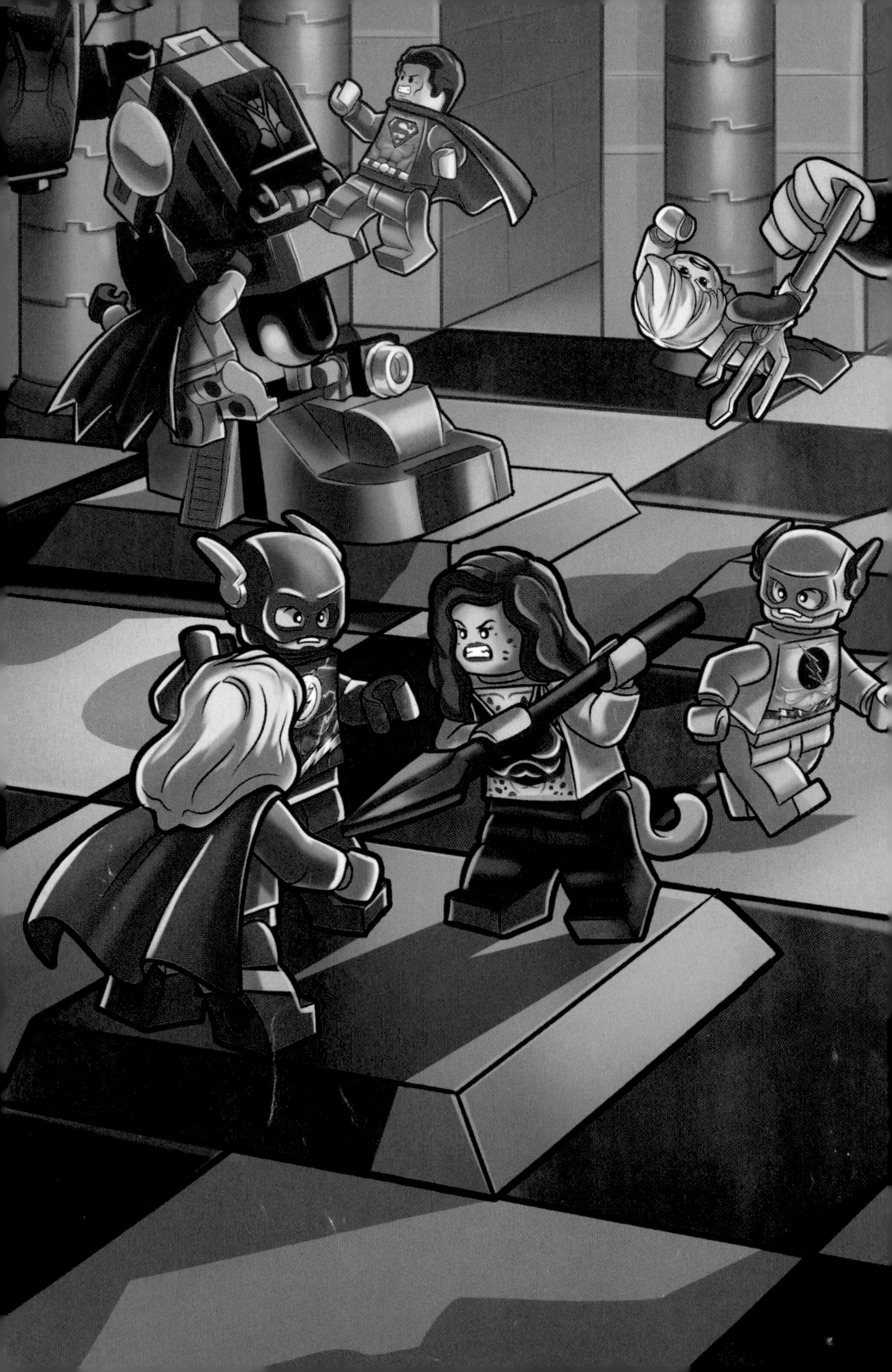

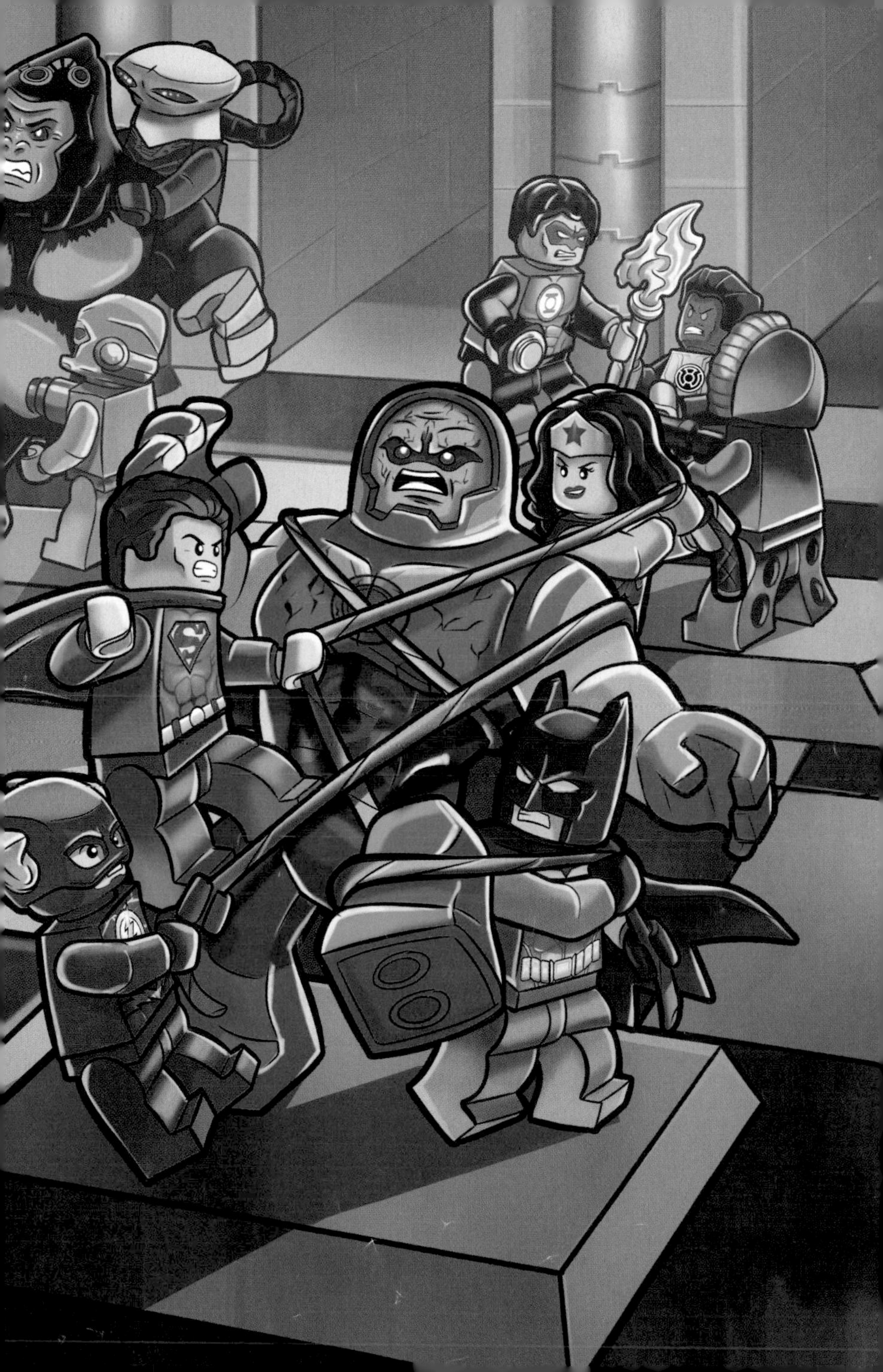

But once inside the hall, Reverse-Flash was forced to slow down and look around carefully. All around him were life-sized statues of heroes fighting various villains. They looked totally real! The real Flash had to be somewhere in here . . . but where? He passed one display of The Flash fighting Cheetah. Another showed The Flash fighting Killer Frost.

Reverse-Flash kept walking, looking all around him. "Wait a minute," muttered Reverse-Flash. "Why are there *two* Flashes here? There's only one statue of every other character in here!" He shoved past the Killer Frost statue and punched The Flash statue as hard as he could. *CRUNCH!* His fist smashed into hard stone.

"Ow!" he complained, shaking out his hand. He looked at the second Flash in the display, the one fighting Cheetah.

The Flash blinked and grinned. "That sounds like my cue!" He laughed. "Do you know how *hard* it is for me to hold still for that long? Catch me outside!" He raced out of the exhibit.

"Get back here!" shouted Reverse-Flash. He chased The Flash across the entrance hall and through a door marked MIRROR MAZE. As he went inside, he saw that all around him were mirrors, forming narrow halls that led in every direction. "WHERE ARE YOU?" he howled. Reverse-Flash started breaking the mirrors, one by one.

"Yikes!" The Flash yelled. He rushed out of the maze and up the stairs to the second floor. Reverse-Flash followed, and the two began running circles in super-speed, around and around the museum.

"Whew," said The Flash. "This is making me dizzy!"

"Then stop," came Batgirl's voice over the communicator. "We're ready for you out here."

"Perfect!" The Flash ran out into the entrance hall. Reverse-Flash was right behind him as they charged outside.

Batman, Batgirl, Superman, and Supergirl were waiting for them. They had rebuilt and rewired the robot parts from the robot ghosts into a glowing cage right outside the front door.

As The Flash threw the door open, Supergirl swooped down and yanked him into the air, out of the way.

Reverse-Flash had no time to stop. He ran straight into the cage, and Superman slammed the door shut behind him.

VMMMMMMMMMMMM! The cage powered up and glowed even brighter. Reverse-Flash tried to spin around quickly . . . but he just turned at normal speed. He looked down at himself in shock.

"That's right," Batgirl told him. "We built this cage from your tech, and we built it to take away your powers."

Batman nodded with satisfaction. "Looks like Central City is safe from all evildoers—"

"Including robot ghosts from the future!" interrupted The Flash.

Batman grunted and continued. ". . . All evildoers *including robot ghosts from the future,* thanks to the Justice League!"

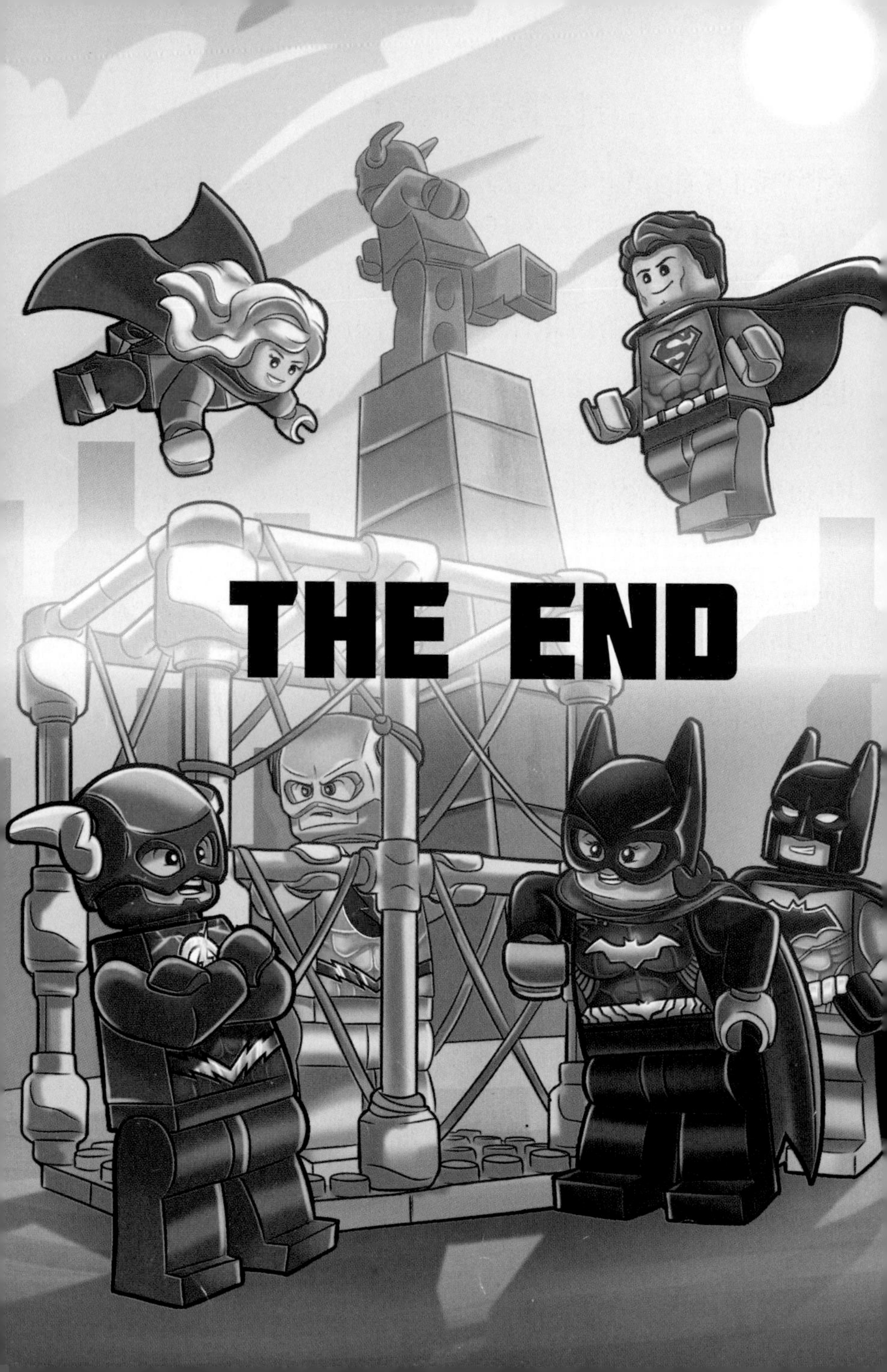
THE END

GLOSSARY

ANTENNA: A metallic device (such as a rod or wire) for radiating or receiving radio waves.

BATGIRL: A Super Hero who lives in Gotham City, Barbara Gordon fights crime as Batgirl.

BATMAN: A Super Hero who lives in Gotham City. Batman is really Bruce Wayne.

CENTRAL CITY: The city where The Flash and Captain Cold live.

CHEETAH: A half-woman, half-cheetah super-villain with super-speed and super-strength.

COMMUNICATOR: A device Super Heroes use to talk to one another from far away.

COSMIC TREADMILL: A time-travel machine used by The Flash.

EXHIBIT: A collection of art or historical artifacts put on display.

THE FLASH: A Super Hero who has the power to run, think, and talk very fast.

FLASH MUSEUM: A museum in Central City all about The Flash, his friends, and his enemies.

FOOTAGE: Another name for a video.

HALL OF HEROES: A section of the Flash Museum that has real-looking statues of heroes and villains.

HEAT VISION: A superpower that lets heroes shoot hot beams out of their eyes.

JUSTICE LEAGUE: A team of Super Heroes. Batman, Superman, Supergirl, Aquaman, Green Lantern, The Flash, and Batgirl are all part of the Justice League.

KILLER FROST: A super-villain who can absorb heat and project cold and ice.

MANSION: A very large house.

REVERSE-FLASH: An evil scientist from the future with the same powers as The Flash.

SUPERGIRL: A Super Hero who has super-strength and super-speed like her cousin, Superman.

SUPERMAN: A Super Hero who can fly, heat things with his eyes, and cool things with his breath, and is super-strong.